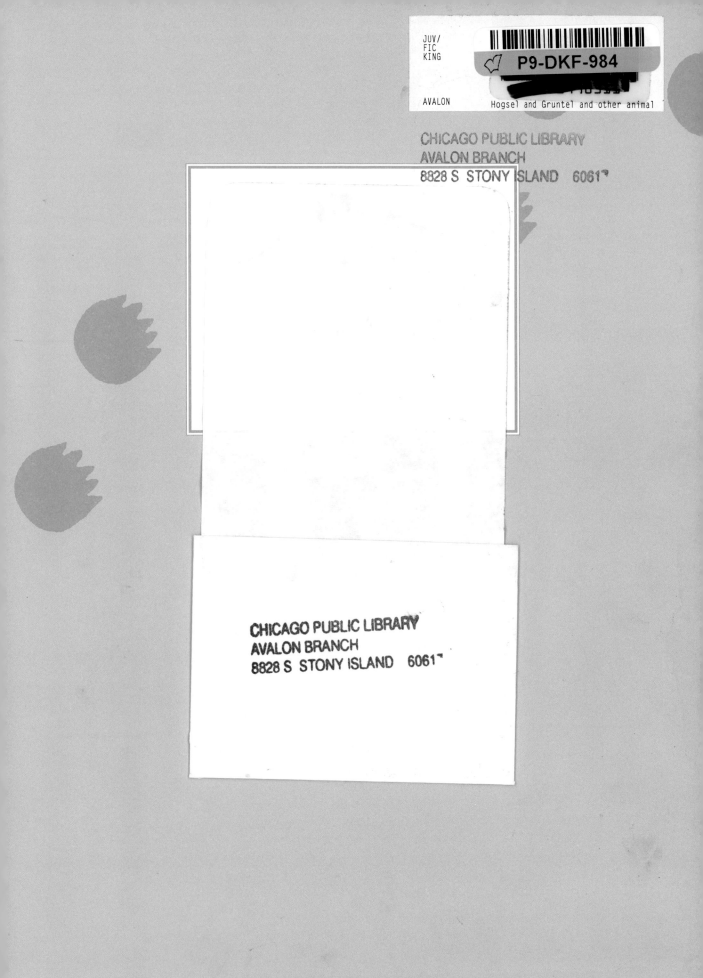

Hogsel and Gruntel

AND

Other Animal Stories

DICK KING-SMITH

Illustrated by Michael Terry

ORCHARD BOOKS   NEW YORK

First American edition 1999 published by Orchard Books
First published in Great Britain in 1999 by the Penguin Group under the title *More Animal Stories*

"Poppet," "The Spelling Bee," and "The Septopus" copyright © 1999 by Fox Busters Ltd

"Little Red Riding Pig," "The Owl and the Pussy-cat," "Goldipig and the Three Bears,"
"Hogsel and Gruntel," and "The Princess and the Pig" were first published in 1991 by Victor Gollancz Ltd in
Dick King-Smith's *Triffic Pig Book,* copyright © 1991 by Fox Busters Ltd

"Dumpling" was first published in 1986 by Hamish Hamilton Ltd, copyright © 1986 by Dick King-Smith

"Dinosaur School" (under the title "Use Your Brains") and "Norty Boy" were first published in 1993
by Viking in *A Narrow Squeak and Other Animal Stories,* copyright © 1993 by Fox Busters Ltd

"The Ugly Duckling" was first published in 1992 by Victor Gollancz Ltd in *The Topsy-Turvy Storybook,*
copyright © 1992 by Fox Busters Ltd

"The Great Sloth Race" copyright © 1994 by Fox Busters Ltd

"Blessu" was first published in 1990 by Hamish Hamilton Ltd, copyright © 1990 by Fox Busters Ltd

"Zap!" copyright © 1987 by Dick King-Smith

Illustrations copyright © 1999 by Michael Terry

Dick King-Smith and Michael Terry assert the moral right to
be identified as the author and the illustrator of this work.

Orchard Books, A Grolier Company
95 Madison Avenue, New York, NY 10016

Printed at Oriental Press, Dubai, U.A.E
Electronic layout and composition by Helene Berinsky

1 3 5 7 9 10 8 6 4 2

The text of this book is set in 16 point Bembo.

Library of Congress Cataloging-in-Publication Data
King-Smith, Dick.
Hogsel and Gruntel and other animal stories / by Dick King-Smith;
illustrated by Michael Terry. — 1st American ed.
p.   cm.
Summary: Fifteen stories about an assortment of animals, including "Poppet," "The Spelling Bee,"
"The Great Sloth Race," "Norty Boy," and "The Princess and the Pig."
ISBN 0-531-30208-3 (alk. paper)
1. Animals—Juvenile fiction. 2. Children's stories, English. [1. Animals—Fiction. 2. Short stories.]
I. Terry, Michael, ill. II. Title.   PZ7.K5893Ho   1999   [Fic]—dc21   99-21446

Contents

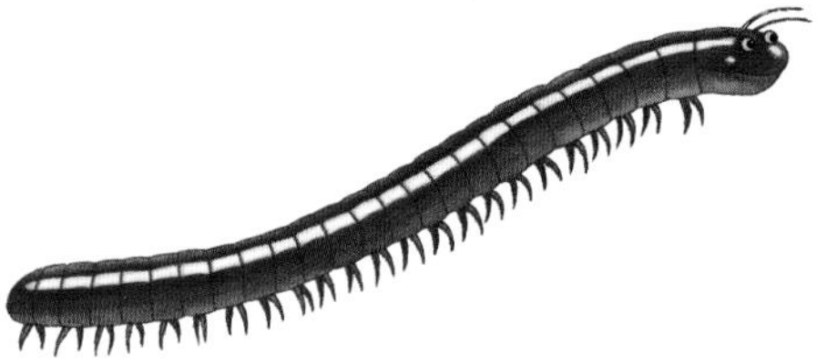

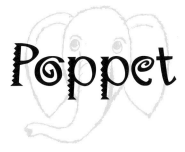

Poppet

When Poppet was born, he had absolutely no idea what sort of animal he was.

He looked around and saw that he was surrounded by a forest of legs. Huge legs they were, thick and tall and grayish in color, with huge feet on the ends of them.

Poppet looked up and saw, on top of all those legs, huge bodies with huge heads and huge ears and amazingly long, long noses.

He was, in fact, looking up at his mother and a number of his aunts, who had all come along to inspect this new baby.

"Oh!" said one aunt. "Isn't he a poppet!"

The baby's mother looked extremely pleased.

"What are you going to call him?" said another aunt.

The baby's mother, whose own name was Ooma, said, "I don't know. I haven't had time to think." And then she thought for a bit and said, "But now I do know. I'll call him Poppet." She put the tip of her trunk against one of the baby's ears and whispered, "Hello, baby. I'm your mom, and your name is Poppet."

Poppet looked up at Ooma and the other huge animals and said, "Please, what sort of animals are you?"

"Elephants," said Ooma. "We are African elephants."

"Oh," said Poppet. "But you said you were my mom."

"Yes."

"So does that make me an African elephant?"

"Yes."

Poppet looked puzzled. There must be some mistake, he thought. "You're enormous," he said, "and I'm very small. We can't be the same sort of animal."

"Oh yes we are," said Ooma. "It's just that you're a baby elephant."

"But you'll grow," said one of the aunts.

"And grow," said another.

"And grow."

"And grow."

"And grow," said all the others.

"Until you're as big as we are," said Ooma. "You might even be bigger one day."

"Tomorrow?" said Poppet.

At this the aunts all laughed quietly, making snuffly noises in their trunks, before moving slowly and heavily away, leaving mother and baby alone together.

"No, not tomorrow, Poppet," said Ooma gently. "Elephants take a long, long time to grow to full size. But you'll get there one day. There's nothing to stop you, for we are too big and our skins are too thick for any other creature in Africa to hurt us. Except two."

"What are they, Mom?" asked Poppet.

"One," said Ooma, "is a monkeylike thing called a man. Men kill elephants."

"Why?"

"For our tusks."

"What are tusks?"

"Great big, long teeth that elephants have. Like these two of mine."

"I haven't got any."

"You will. But you should be all right, because we live in a special place called a reserve, where elephants are protected."

"Oh," said Poppet. "But you said there were *two* creatures that could hurt us. What's the other one, besides a man?"

"A mouse," said Ooma.

"Oh," said Poppet. "Are they even bigger and stronger than us, these mouses?"

"Mice," said Ooma, "are very small, and, what's more, mice live in holes, and that's the trouble."

She stretched out her long, long trunk till the tip of it was right in front of Poppet's face.

"What do you see, Poppet?" she said.

"A hole," said Poppet.

Then Ooma, speaking slowly and solemnly, repeated to her newborn child the old elephant-wives' tale that her mother had told her when she was a baby, a tale in which she had always believed.

"Poppet, my son," she said. "First, never have anything to do with mice. Second, if you should be unfortunate enough to meet one, keep your trunk curled up out of the way. Never, never put the tip of it anywhere near a mouse, otherwise the most dreadful thing imaginable will happen to you."

"What's that?" said Poppet.

"The mouse will run up the inside of your trunk."

Poppet thought about this for the rest of the first day of his life.

He imagined this thing called a mouse running along inside his little trunk and he did not like the thought of it at all. Suppose one did! How would he get rid of it? Blow it out, he supposed. Every so often for the remainder of the day, he blew very hard, suddenly, down his trunk, just in case one of the awful creatures had somehow crept in.

I don't even know what they look like, he thought, only that they're small.

The next morning while the elephant herd was browsing upon the leaves of some large trees, Poppet was standing beside his mother when he saw a strange animal moving around on the bark of one of the trees.

What it was he didn't know, but it was certainly small.

Carefully curling his trunk up out of harm's way, Poppet bent his head toward it. Close up he could see that the creature, though small, was long, with a great many joints to its dark brown body and many legs. Perfect for crawling up elephants' trunks, he thought. I bet you are one. He said politely, "Excuse me, but are you a mouse?"

"A mouse?" said the creature.

"Yes. I thought you might be."

"You're joking! Pull the other one."

"Other what?"

"Leg."

What does it mean? Poppet thought. It's got hundreds of legs. "Well, if you're not a mouse," he said, "what are you?"

"I'm a giant millipede," said the long, wriggly creature.

"A giant!" said Poppet.

8

"Oh, stop joking around," said the millipede huffily. "You knew all the time, didn't you? I could tell—I wasn't born yesterday."

"I was," said Poppet, as the giant millipede rippled away.

"But anyway, I've learned something. That animal was not a mouse."

In the days and weeks that followed, he asked quite a number of small creatures whether they were mice. He asked beetles and grubs and worms and caterpillars and little lizards and small frogs, and some replied jokily and some replied angrily and some didn't answer. At last Poppet rather forgot about his mother's dire warning and gave himself up to enjoying the carefree life of a baby elephant. He used his trunk for reaching up and pulling down leaves and twigs, and for sucking up water when the herd went to

9

the river to drink, and then for blowing water all over himself. When he was nice and wet, he would go to a dusty place and use his trunk to give himself a dust bath, so that he finished up beautifully muddy. Then he'd go back into the river and have a lovely swim, going right under the water with just the tip of his trunk sticking up above the surface like a snorkel.

A trunk, Poppet decided, was a wonderful thing to have. As for mice, he never thought about them anymore.

Then one hot afternoon when he was about a month old

10

and his mother and all the aunts were standing resting in the shade, Poppet wandered off a little way, exploring.

He was using his trunk to search about in the grass as he went along, when suddenly he saw in front of him an animal that he had not previously met. It was furry and brown, with large tulip-shaped ears, beady black eyes, and a longish hairless tail, and Poppet stretched out his trunk toward it and sniffed at it.

Even when the tip of his trunk was right in front of the creature's face, it didn't occur to him that this animal was small, and—without much hope because he'd been wrong so many times—he said, "Are you a mouse?"

"As a matter of fact," said the animal, "I am. And you know what mice do to elephants, don't you?"

Poppet hastily raised his trunk.

"Aha!" said the mouse. "Your mom told you, did she?"

"Told me what?"

"That mice run up inside elephants' trunks."

"Well, yes," said Poppet. "She did."

"And you believed her?"

"Yes."

The mouse let out a loud squeak, whether of anger or of fright Poppet did not know (in fact, it was of delight).

"What are you called, boy?" it said.

"Poppet. What about you?"

"My name," said the mouse, "is Momo, and I am very glad to meet you."

"Oh," said Poppet. "Why?"

"Because," said Momo, "when I was very young, my mother told me this story about mice and elephants, and I didn't believe her. That's rubbish, I thought. One day, I said to myself, I'll meet an elephant and find out if it's true. And now I've met one."

"But you're not going to find out," said Poppet, and he curled his trunk even higher.

"Oh, come on!" said Momo. "Be a sport. Just let me have a look up it."

"No, no!" cried Poppet. "You'll crawl in."

"I won't, honest."

"Promise?"

"Cross my heart."

So, very slowly, Poppet uncurled his trunk and lowered the tip of it toward the waiting mouse. The nearer it got to Momo, the more nervous Poppet became. I must be crazy, he thought, believing a mouse's promise. Mice probably don't know the meaning of *promise*.

Then suddenly he felt the tickle of whiskers at the very tip of his trunk as Momo peered into it, and he gave an enormous sneeze.

13

Elephants, like people, shut their eyes when they sneeze, and when Poppet opened his again, it was to see that the mouse had been blown head over heels by the force of the blast.

"Whoa!" cried Momo. "What are you doing?"

"Sorry," said Poppet. "I sneezed."

"Oh. Well, bless you."

"Thanks. It was your whiskers. They tickled."

"Just testing. A mouse can go into any hole that's wider than its whiskers."

"And was it?"

"It would have been a very tight fit," said Momo. "Might be possible with a full-grown elephant, but I wouldn't have cared to try it with you, Poppet my lad. Anyway, to be quite frank, it looked pretty damp and uninviting up there, even before the sneeze. As it is, I'm soaked."

"I'll dry you," said Poppet, and he pointed his trunk at the mouse and blew long, slow, hot breaths over him.

It was while he was doing this that he suddenly heard his mother's voice, and a very angry voice it was. Ooma had walked up behind him quite silently, as elephants do on their great cushioned feet, only to see her son with his trunk outstretched, the tip of it just inches from a mouse!

She let out a furious trumpet, and Momo vanished from sight.

"What did I tell you?" screamed Ooma. "Keep away from mice, d'you hear me? Get out of my way now, and I'll squash this one flat."

"Oh, don't, Mom!" cried Poppet. "He's my friend!"

"Your friend!" snorted Ooma. "You're not just a bad child, you're a crazy child." And she went stamping about in the grass till she'd flattened a big patch of it.

"That should have fixed the horrid creature," she said, and she moved away to rejoin the herd, grumbling to herself.

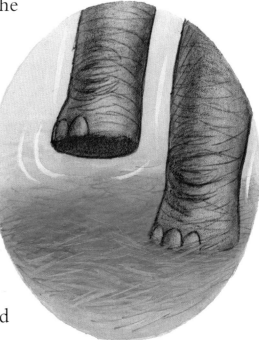

Poppet stood sadly beside the trampled patch.

"Alas, poor mouse!" he said. "It's all my fault that he's dead."

"No, he isn't," said a voice, and

out of the grass poked a little brown head, whiskers twitching.

"Momo!" cried Poppet. "You're not hurt?"

"Got a bit of a headache."

"How on earth did you survive?"

"Underground. Went down a hole quick as a wink," said the mouse. "But not before I heard what you said. Which was nice of you, Poppet. You are my friend too."

Meanwhile Ooma was telling the aunts about her naughty child.

"One of the first things I told him," she said, "was to keep away from mice. We all know that every mouse is just waiting for a chance to run up the inside of our trunks."

"We do," said the aunts.

"And no doubt you all gave your kids the same warning."

"We did," said the aunts.

"And what have I just found? Only my boy with the tip of his trunk right beside a mouse, that's all. I told him off, I can tell you. No doubt you'd have done the same?"

"We would," said the aunts.

"Children!" said Ooma. "They just don't listen."

"Grown-ups!" Poppet said to Momo at about the same time. "They don't treat children fairly, grown-ups don't. I could have explained to Mom if she'd let me. I could have told her, 'You're wrong. Mice don't run up elephants' trunks. I know. My friend told me.' But no, I never got the chance. She just yelled at me."

"I heard it," said Momo.

"Let's just hope we're more understanding when we're grown-ups," said Poppet.

"Actually," said Momo, "I'm a grown-up already."

"Oh, sorry! I didn't realize. You're so . . . um . . ."

"Small?"

"Well, yes."

"Tell you what, Poppet," said the mouse. "Do you agree that it would be a good thing if elephants stopped being frightened of mice?"

"Yes, I do."

"And do you agree that it would be a good thing if elephants stopped trying to squash mice?"

"Oh, yes, I do."

"All right, then. This is my plan. Listen carefully."

And so it was that later that day, when the herd had been down to the river to bathe and the elephants were all standing in the shade, resting, Poppet said to Ooma, "Mom, will you promise not to yell at me if I tell you something?"

"Of course I won't," said Ooma, who was already rather ashamed of losing her temper with her little one.

"Of course you won't promise?"

"No. Of course I won't yell at you."

"All right, then," said Poppet. "It's this. Mice do *not* run

up inside elephants' trunks. They never have and they never will."

Ooma snorted.

"Come and listen to this," she called to the aunts, and when they had all gathered around, she made Poppet repeat his words.

"Silly boy," said one aunt, and "Stupid child," said another, and a third said, "You had a narrow escape this morning. You might not be so lucky another time."

"Wait here, please," said Poppet, and he disappeared into

some bushes. When he emerged again, Ooma and the aunts could see that he was holding something in the tip of his trunk, something furry and brown, with large tulip-shaped ears, beady black eyes, and a longish hairless tail—a mouse!

How horrified they all were! They formed a circle around Poppet, their trunks held high out of the reach of the dreaded creature that he carried, and they shifted anxiously from foot to foot, fanning their great ears.

Poppet put the mouse carefully down upon the ground.

"This is Momo," he said to Ooma and the aunts. "My friend, like I told you, Mom. I know I am only a child, but Momo is a grown-up, even though you may think he's not grown very far. However, he has a grown-up brain, I can tell you, and he wishes to address you all, if you will be kind enough to listen to him."

So astonished were the elephants, first to see Poppet carrying the mouse, and then to hear him make such a speech, that they stopped fidgeting and stood silent, except for the rumbling of their tummies, which they couldn't help.

Momo sat up on his haunches.

"Ladies," he said. "It is a great privilege to be allowed to speak to you, and"—he turned to face Ooma—"especially you, madam, the mother of a truly remarkable child."

Elephants can't blush, but if Ooma could have, she would have.

"Poppet," the mouse went on, "is a name that all elephants will remember for all time, since it is he—with a little help from myself—who has been the first of his kind to discover that mice do *not*, never have, and never will run up the inside of elephants' trunks. I call upon him now to conclude this historic day by offering to all of you the proof

of what I have just said. So that none of you here, indeed none of your kind throughout the length and breadth of Africa, need ever again worry about meeting a mouse, trunk to face. Now, Poppet, say your piece."

"Mom," said Poppet, "do you love me?"

"Oh, yes, Poppet," said Ooma.

"Would you do anything for me?"

"Oh, yes."

"Then uncurl your trunk and stretch out the tip of it to Momo."

"Oh, no, Poppet! I couldn't!"

"Courage, madam," said Momo, while all the aunts cried, "Go on, Ooma!" safe in the knowledge that they didn't have to do it.

"It'll be all right, Mom," said Poppet. "Honest."

So very slowly, with her eyes tightly shut, Ooma uncoiled her trunk and laid the tip of it on the ground, right beside the mouse. Momo peered up it, careful (remembering Poppet's sneeze) not to touch it with his whiskers.

"Yuck!" he said softly.

Then he said to Ooma, "Thank you, madam. I appreciate

your confidence and your courage, and I am filled with admiration for the undoubted beauty, strength, and dexterity of your magnificent nasal appendage. I hope, however, that you will forgive me if I say that nothing in this world could ever persuade me to creep up your trunk."

"I had a hard time keeping a straight face," said Momo after the herd had moved away, shaking their great heads in wonder at what they had just seen and heard. Ooma especially had seemed quite overcome by what had happened, and when Poppet had said to her, "Mom, can I

stay and play with Momo?" she had answered, "Yes, of course, dear," as though hypnotized.

When they were alone, Poppet said, "What shall we play? Can you think of a game?"

"Yes," said Momo. "Put down your trunk and I'll run up it."

"Oh, no!" cried Poppet. "You mean it's true after all, what Mom told me? And I thought you were my friend!"

"I am," said Momo. "Don't get your trunk all bent out of shape. I just want to run up the *outside*."

Little Red Riding Pig

Little Red Riding Pig set out one day to visit her grandmother. She was called Little Red Riding Pig because she was small, of a reddish color, and always rode around on her mountain bike.

Cycling through a forest glade, she met a wolf.

"Hold it right there, baby," said the wolf.

Little Red Riding Pig held it.

"Where you headin'?" said the wolf.

"To visit my grandmother," replied Little Red Riding Pig.

The wolf thought quickly. Not a lot of meat on this

piglet, he said to himself, but the granny—now she might make a square meal.

"Your granny kinda fat?" he asked in a casual way.

"Oh yes!" said Little Red Riding Pig. "She's very fat."

"Sure like to meet her," said the wolf. "She live around here someplace?"

"Oh, yes!" said Little Red Riding Pig, and she told the wolf how to get to her grandmother's house, and away he went.

When he arrived, he knocked on the door, and a voice called, "Come in, my dear," so he did.

There, lying in bed, was the fattest pig the wolf had ever seen.

"Goodness me!" said the pig. "I thought you were my little granddaughter."

"'Fraid not, ma'am," said the wolf.

"But I see now," said Little Red Riding Pig's grandmother, "that you are in fact a handsome stranger. What big ears you have!"

All the better to hear you with, thought the wolf, but he kept his mouth shut.

"And what big eyes you have!"

All the better to see you with, thought the wolf, but he said nothing, merely opening his jaws in a kind of silent laugh.

"And what big teeth you have!" said the fat pig, and before the wolf could think about that, she went on, "Which reminds me, I have a toothache. I would be so grateful if you could look and see which tooth is causing the trouble."

"Why sure, ma'am," said the wolf, and he approached the bed, drooling slightly at the thought of the feast in store.

The fat pig opened her mouth wide, and the wolf bent his head to look into it.

Not long afterward Little Red Riding Pig came pedaling up on her mountain bike. Usually when she knocked on the door, her grandmother would call, "Come in, my dear," but now all Little Red Riding Pig heard was a grunt.

She opened the door.

Her grandmother looked even fatter than usual. And there was something else odd about her.

"Why, Granny," cried Little Red Riding Pig in amazement, "you have grown a long, gray beard!"

But it was only the wolf's tail, still sticking out of her grandmother's mouth.

◢◣

The Owl and the Pussycat

You all know that the Owl and the Pussycat went to

sea in a beautiful pea-green boat. But do you remember

the Piggy-wig they met in a wood with a ring

at the end of his nose? And do you ever wonder

what he did with the shilling that they gave him?

Well, read on. . . .

Said the Piggy, "I will."

"At last," said the Piggy-wig, "I can rootle!"

Rootling in the ground with their strong snouts is something all pigs love doing, but they cannot rootle if they have rings in their noses.

29

"At last," said the Piggy-wig again, "I am rid of that horrid ring. And what's more, that Owl and that Pussycat actually paid me for it! A whole shilling! Though I do not know what on earth to do with it. But talking of earth gives me an idea"—and he dug a little hole with his snout and buried the shilling in a safe place, under the Bong-Tree. Then off he went all around the wood, rootling and rootling to his heart's content.

He had turned up all sorts of nice things—bulbs and roots and beetles—when suddenly his snout struck upon something hard. It was a large spoon, whose handle had been bent at right angles to its bowl by the force of the pig's rootling.

At that moment the Turkey who lives on the hill came strutting by.

"That spoon won't be much use to you at the wedding feast," he said.

"I haven't been asked," said the Pig.

"Pity," said the Turkey. "They're having mince. And slices of quince."

The Pig licked his lips.

"I could get you an invite," said the Turkey.

"Could you?" said the Pig eagerly.

"At a price."

"How much?"

"One shilling."

"Done!" said the Pig, and he rushed back to the Bong-Tree and dug up his shilling and gave it to the Turkey.

The next day the Owl and the Pussycat were married by the Turkey who lives on the hill. All the invited guests (including the Pig) were there, and all had brought wedding presents (except the Pig).

"What can I give them?" he whispered anxiously to the Turkey, who snickered and replied, "Give 'em that old spoon."

Quickly, for he did not want to miss the wedding feast, the Pig ran back to the wood and found the spoon.

When he returned with it, he could see that something was wrong. The Pussycat was in tears, the Owl was trying to comfort her, and the guests were tut-tutting and dear-dearing among themselves.

"All ruined!" cried the Pussycat. "All wasted!"

"O lovely Pussy!" said the Owl. "Whatever's the matter?"

"Mince!" cried the Pussycat. "And slices of quince! There's only one possible way to eat them, and that we cannot do!"

At this moment the Piggy-wig pushed his way through the crowd of guests and dropped before the unhappy couple the large spoon with the right-angled handle.

"Hope you'll be very happy," he said gruffly.

"O Piggy-wig!" cried the Pussycat, drying her tears. "Now we most certainly shall be! Your wedding present is the one thing that we needed, the one thing without which it is not possible to dine on mince and slices of quince!"

"O Pussy, my love!" said the Owl, looking in puzzlement at the Piggy-wig's present. "What is it?"

"You elegant fowl!" laughed the Pussycat joyfully. "It's a runcible spoon!"

Dumpling

 h, how I long to be long!" said Dumpling.

"Who do you want to belong to?" asked one of her brothers.

"No, I don't mean to belong," said Dumpling. "I mean, *be long!*"

When the three dachshund puppies were born, they had looked much like pups of any other breed.

Then, as they became older, the two brothers began to grow long, as dachshunds do. Their noses moved further and further away from their tail tips.

But the third puppy stayed short and stumpy.

"How long you are getting," said the lady who owned them all to the two brothers.

She called one of them Joker because he was always playing silly games, and the other one Thinker because he liked to sit and think deeply.

Then she looked at their sister and shook her head.

"You are nice and healthy," she said. "Your eyes are bright and your coat is shining, and you're good and plump. But dachshunds are supposed to have long bodies, you know. And you don't. You're just a little dumpling."

Dumpling asked her mother about the problem.

36

"Will I ever grow really long like Joker and Thinker?" she asked.

Her mother looked at her plump daughter and sighed.

"Time will tell," she said.

Dumpling asked her brother Joker.

"Joker," she said, "how can I grow longer?"

"That's easy, Dumpy," said Joker. "I'll hold your nose, and Thinker will hold your tail, and we'll stretch you."

"Don't be silly, Joker," said Thinker.

Thinker was a serious puppy. He did not like to play jokes. "It would hurt Dumpy if we did that."

"Well then, what shall I do, Thinker?" asked Dumpling.

Thinker thought deeply. Then he said, "Try going for long walks. And it helps if you take very long steps."

So Dumpling set off the next morning. All of the dachshunds were out in the garden. The puppies' mother was snoozing in the sunshine.

Joker was playing a silly game pretending that a stick was a snake.

Thinker was sitting and thinking deeply.

Dumpling slipped away through a hole in the hedge.

Next to the garden was a forest, and she set off among the trees on her very short legs. She stepped out boldly, trying hard to imagine herself growing a tiny bit longer with each step.

Suddenly she bumped into a large black cat who was sitting under a yew tree.

"Oh, I beg your pardon!" said Dumpling.

"Granted," said the cat. "Where are you going?"

"Oh, nowhere special. I'm just taking a long walk. You see, I'm trying to grow longer." She went on to explain about dachshunds and how they should look.

"Everyone calls me Dumpling," she said sadly. "I wish I could be long."

"Granted," said the black cat again.

"What do you mean?" Dumpling said. "Can you make me long?"

"Easy as winking," said the cat, winking. "I'm a witch's cat. I'll cast a spell on you. How long do you want to be?"

"Oh, very, very long!" cried Dumpling excitedly. "The longest dachshund ever!"

The black cat stared at her with his green eyes, and then he shut them and began to chant:

> *"Abra-cat-abra,*
> *hark to my song.*
> *It will make you*
> *very long."*

The sound of the cat's voice died away, and the forest was suddenly very still.

Then the cat gave himself a shake and opened his eyes.

"Remember," he said, "you asked for it."

"Oh, thank you, thank you!" said Dumpling. "I feel longer already. Will I see you again?"

"I shouldn't be surprised," said the cat.

Dumpling set off back toward the garden. The feeling of growing longer was lovely. She wagged her tail wildly, and each wag seemed a little farther away than the last.

She thought how surprised Joker and Thinker would be. She would be much longer than them.

"Dumpling, indeed!" she said. "I will have to have a new name now, a very long one to match my new body."

But then she began to find walking difficult. Her front feet knew where they were going, but her back feet acted very oddly. They seemed to be a long way behind her.

They kept tripping over things and dropping into rabbit holes.

They kept getting stuck among the bushes. She couldn't see her tail, so she went around a big tree to look for it and met it on the other side.

By now she was wriggling on her tummy like a snake.

40

"Help!" yapped Dumpling at the top of her voice. "Cat, come back, please!"

"Granted," said the witch's cat, appearing suddenly beside her. "What's the trouble now?"

"Oh, please," cried Dumpling, "undo your spell!"

"Some people are never satisfied," said the cat. Once more he stared at her with his green eyes.

Then he shut them and began to chant:

> *"Abra-cat-abra,*
> *hear my song.*
> *It will make you*
> *short, not long."*

Dumpling never forgot how wonderful it felt as her back feet came toward her front ones, and her tummy rose from the ground.

She hurried homeward and squeezed her nice, comfortable, short, stumpy body through the hole in the hedge.

Joker and Thinker came galloping across the grass toward her.

How clumsy they look, she thought, with those silly long bodies.

"Where have you been, Dumpy?" shouted Joker.

"Did the exercise make you longer?" asked Thinker.

"No," said Dumpling. "But as a matter of fact, I'm quite happy as I am now. And that's about the long and the short of it!"

Goldipig and the Three Bears

Goldipig was a very inquisitive little swine, always poking her snout into other people's business.

Rooting around in the forest one day, she came upon a house among the trees. "I wonder who lives there?" said Goldipig, and when she had called "Hello!" and no one had answered, she pushed the door open and went in.

The first thing she saw was a table with three chairs around it: one big, one ordinary-sized, one little. And on the table in front of each chair was a bowl of porridge: one big, one ordinary-sized, one little.

Goldipig gobbled up all the porridge.

Then, nosy as ever, she trotted upstairs. There in a bedroom were three beds: one big, one ordinary-sized, one little.

"I'll have a nap," said Goldipig, feeling rather full.

She tried each bed in turn. The first was too little, the second too ordinary, but the third, the big bed, was just right, so Goldipig snuggled down and went to sleep.

Shortly afterward the owners of the house returned. They had been taking a walk to work up an appetite for breakfast. They were, in fact, three bears: one big, one ordinary-sized, one little.

"Who's been sitting on our chairs?" said the little bear.

"And where's our porridge gone?" said the ordinary-sized bear.

"And who," said the big bear, listening carefully, "is that snoring upstairs?"

Very quietly the three bears climbed to the bedroom and looked in and saw Goldipig.

"She's messed up all our beds," said the little bear.

"After eating all our porridge," said the ordinary-sized bear.

"And so," said the big bear, "we'll just have to eat her."

At that, Goldipig let out an enormous squeal, dashed past the bears, and rushed downstairs and away. So you can see the three of them got neither porridge nor ham for their breakfast!

The Spelling Bee

For weeks Noah's Ark had been sailing around on the great waters of the Flood, and all of the animals were getting very bored.

Noah noticed this.

"They haven't got enough to do," he said to Mrs. Noah. "They need to use their brains. We'll have a competition."

"What sort of competition?" asked Mrs. Noah.

Noah thought for a bit, and then he said, "A spelling competition.

"We're going to have a spelling competition," he told all

the animals, "to see who is the cleverest among you. Who would like to take part?"

One of the two elephants pushed forward.

"I am the biggest animal in the Ark," it said, "so it stands to reason that I must be the cleverest. What do you want me to spell?"

"Your name," said Noah.

"That's easy," said the elephant. "E . . . L . . . L . . ."

"Stop!" said Noah. "I'm afraid you're spelling that wrong. Next, please."

"I am the tallest animal in the Ark," said one of the two giraffes, "so it stands to reason that *I* must be the cleverest. What do you want me to spell?"

"Your name," said Noah.

"That's easy," said the giraffe. "J . . . I . . . R . . ."

"Hold it!" said Noah. "I'm afraid you're spelling that wrong. Next, please."

"I have the thickest skin of any of the animals in the Ark," said one of the two rhinoceroses, "so it stands to reason that *I* must be the cleverest. What do you want me to spell?"

"Your name," said Noah again.

"That's easy," said the rhinoceros. "R . . . I . . . N . . ."

"Hang on!" said Noah. "I'm afraid you're spelling that wrong. Next, please."

Then one of the two monkeys scampered up.

"I must be the cleverest," it said. "The others didn't know what you wanted them to spell, but I do. You want me to spell my name."

"Go on, then," said Noah.

"It couldn't be simpler," said the monkey. "M . . . U . . . N . . ."

"Whoa!" said Noah. "You're wrong too. In fact, it's beginning to look as though there isn't one animal that can spell its name correctly. Does anyone else want to try?"

At that moment one of the two bees on board the Ark came flying along and chanced to land on Noah's hand.

"Ah-ha!" said Noah. "Here's someone else wanting to take part in our competition."

"Who, me?" said the bee.

"Yes, you," said Noah.

"But I'm no good at spelling," said the bee.

"Oh, go on!" said Noah. "Have a try. Tell us how you spell your name."

"My name?" said the bee.

"Yes."

"Bee?" said the bee.

"Yes!" cried Noah. "That's right. B. Go on."

The bee sat silent, so Noah gave it a little pinch to encourage it. "Eee!" cried the bee.

"Yes," said Noah. "E. Keep going." And he gave it another little pinch.

"Eee!" cried the bee again.

"That's it!" shouted Noah. "You've done it. B . . . E . . . E. You, and you alone, have spelled your name correctly. So you must be the cleverest animal in the Ark."

"Who, me?" said the bee.

"Yes, you," said Noah. "So you can buzz off now."

And then everybody (except the elephant and the giraffe and the rhinoceros and the monkey) gave three hearty cheers for the clever little bee.

◢◣

Dinosaur School

Little Basil Brontosaurus came home from his first morning at play school in floods of tears.

"Whatever's the matter, darling?" said his mother, whose name was Araminta. "Why are you crying?"

"They've been teasing me," sobbed Basil.

"Who have? The other children?"

A variety of little dinosaurs went to the play school. There were diplodocuses, iguanodons, ankylosaurs, and many others. Basil was the only young brontosaurus.

"Yes," sniffed Basil. "They said I was stupid. They said I hadn't got a brain in my head."

At this point Basil's father, a forty-ton brontosaurus who

measured twenty-nine yards from nose to tail tip, came lumbering up through the shallows of the lake in which the family lived.

"Herb!" called Araminta. "Did you hear that? The kids at play school said our Basil hadn't a brain in his head."

Herb considered this while pulling up and swallowing large amounts of waterweed.

"He has," he said at last. "Hasn't he?"

"Of course you have, darling," said Araminta to her little son. "Come along with me now, and dry your tears and listen carefully."

Still sniffling, Basil waded into the lake. He followed his mother to a quiet spot, well away from the other dinosaurs that were feeding around the shallows.

Araminta settled herself where the water was deep enough to help support her enormous bulk.

"Now listen to Mommy, Basil darling," she said. "What I'm about to tell you is a secret. Every brontosaurus that ever hatched is told this secret by his or her mommy or daddy, once he or she is old enough. One day you'll be grown-up, and you'll have a wife of your own, and she'll lay eggs, and then you'll have babies. And when those babies are old enough, they'll have to be told, just like I'm going to tell you."

"Tell me what?" said Basil.

"Promise not to breathe a word of it to the other children?"

"All right. But what is it?"

"It is this," said Araminta. "We have two brains."

"You're joking," said Basil.

"I'm not. Every brontosaurus has two brains: one in its head and one in the middle of its back."

"Wow!" cried Basil. "Well, if I've got two brains and all the other kids have only got one, I must be twice as clever as them."

"You are, darling," said Araminta. "You are. So let's have no more of this silly crybaby nonsense. Next time one of the children teases you, just think to yourself, 'I am twice as clever as you.'"

Not only did Basil think this next morning at play school, but he also thought that he was twice as big as the other children.

"Did you have a nice time?" said Araminta when he came home.

"Smashing," said Basil.

"No tears?"

"Not mine," said Basil cheerfully.

"You didn't tell anyone our secret?"

"Oh, no," said Basil. "I didn't do much talking at all to the other kids. Actions speak louder than words."

Not long after this the play school teacher, an elderly female stegosaur, came to see Herb and Araminta.

"I'm sorry to bother you," she said, "but I'm a little worried about Basil."

"Not been blubbering again, has he?" said Herb.

"Oh, no, he hasn't," said the stegosaur. "In fact, recently he has grown greatly in confidence. At first he was rather nervous, and the other children tended to make fun of him, but they don't anymore. He's twice the boy he was."

"Can't think why," said Herb, but Araminta could.

"Indeed," went on the stegosaur, "I fear that lately he's been throwing his weight around. Boys will be boys, I know, but really Basil has become very rough. Only yesterday I had to send home a baby

brachiosaur with a badly bruised foot and a little trachodont with a black eye. I would be glad if you would speak to Basil about all this."

When the teacher had departed, Araminta said to Herb, "You must have a word with the boy."

"Why?" said Herb.

"You heard what the teacher said. He's been bullying the other children. He's obviously getting above himself."

At this point Basil appeared.

"What did old Steggy want?" he said.

"Tell him, Herb," said Araminta.

"Now look here, my boy," said Herb.

Basil looked.

"You listen to me."

Basil listened, but Herb, Araminta could see, had forgotten what he was supposed to be talking about.

"Your father is very angry with you," she said.

"You have been fighting. At play school."

"That's right," said Herb. "Fighting. At play school. Why?"

"Well, it's like this, Dad," said Basil. "The first day the other kids teased me. They said I didn't have a brain in my head, remember? Then Mom told me I did. And another in the middle of my back. Two brains! So I thought, I'm twice as clever as the rest, as well as twice as big, so why not lean on them a bit? Not my fault if they get under my feet."

"You'd better watch your step," said Herb.

"Daddy's right," said Araminta. "One of these days you'll get into real trouble. Now run along; I want to talk to your father."

"It's all my fault for telling him about having two brains," she said when Basil had gone. "He's too young. My parents didn't tell me till I was nearly grown-up. How did you find out?"

"Oh, I don't know," said Herb. "I guess

I heard some of the guys talking down in the swamp. When I was one of the gang. We used to talk a lot, down in the swamp."

"What about?" asked Araminta.

"Waterweed, mostly," said Herb, and he pulled up a great mouthful and began to chomp.

Not long after this, Basil was expelled.

"I'm sorry," said the elderly stegosaur, "but I can't have the boy in my class any longer. It isn't only his roughness, it's his rudeness. Do you know what he said to me today?"

"No," said Herb.

"What?" asked Araminta.

"He said to me, 'I'm twice as clever as you are.' "

"Is he?" asked Herb.

"Of course he isn't," said Araminta hastily. "He was just being silly and childish. I'm sure he won't be any trouble in the future."

"Not in my play school he won't," said the stegosaur. And then, oddly, she used the very words that Araminta had used earlier: "One of these days," she said, "he'll get into real trouble." And off she waddled, flapping her back plates angrily.

And one of those days, Basil did.

Being expelled from play school hadn't worried him at all. What do I want with other dinosaurs? he thought. I'm far superior to them, with my two brains: one to work my neck and my front legs, one to work my back legs and my tail. Brontosauruses are twice as clever as other dinosaurs, and I'm twice as clever as any other brontosaurus.

You couldn't say that Basil was bigheaded, for that was

almost the smallest part of him, but you could certainly say that he was boastful, conceited, and arrogant.

"That boy!" said Araminta to Herb. "He's boastful, conceited, and arrogant. He must get it from your side of the family, swaggering around and picking fights all the time. What does he think he is? A *Tyrannosaurus rex*?"

"What do you think you are?" Basil was saying at that very moment. He had left the lake where the family spent almost all their time and gone off for a walk.

He had been ambling along, thinking what a fine fellow he was, when suddenly he had seen a strange, smallish dinosaur standing in his path.

It was not like any dinosaur he had ever seen before. It stood upright on its hind legs, which were much bigger than its little forelegs, and it had a large head with large jaws and a great many teeth. But compared to Basil, who already weighed a couple of tons, it looked quite small, and he advanced upon it, saying in a rude tone, "What do you think you are?"

"I'm a *Tyrannosaurus rex,*" said the stranger.

"Never heard of you," said Basil.

64

"Lucky you."

"Why? What's so wonderful about you? You can't even walk on four feet like a decent dinosaur, and you've only got one brain. Next you'll be telling me that you don't eat waterweed like we do."

"We don't," said the other. "We only eat meat."

"What sort of meat?"

"Brontosaurus, mostly."

"Let's get this straight," said Basil. "Are you seriously telling me that you kill brontosauruses and eat them?"

"Yes."

"Don't make me laugh," said Basil. "I'm four times as big as you."

"Yes," said the youngster, "but my dad's four times as big as you. Oh, look, what a bit of luck: here he comes!"

Basil looked up to see a terrifying sight.

Marching toward him on its huge hind legs was a towering, full-grown *Tyrannosaurus rex* with a mouthful of long, razor-sharp teeth. All of a sudden Basil had two brainstorms.

Time I went, he thought. Fast. And as one brain sent a message rippling along to the other, he turned tail and headed for the safety of the lake as fast as his legs could carry him.

This was not very fast, as Basil's big body made him slow and clumsy on land. If the tyrannosaurus had been really hungry, he would have caught Basil without any trouble.

As it was, Basil reached the

shore of the lake just in time and splashed frantically out to deeper water, where his parents, their long necks outstretched, were grazing on the weedy bottom.

Araminta was the first to look up.

"Hello, darling," she said. "Where have you been? Whatever's the matter? You're all in a tizzy."

"Oh, Mommy, Mommy!" panted Basil. "It was awful! I went for a walk and I was nearly eaten by a *Tyrannosaurus rex*!"

Herb raised his head in time to hear this.

"That'll teach you," he said.

"Teach me what, Dad?"

"Not to be so cocky," said Araminta. "Ever since I told you that secret, you've been unbearable, Basil. I hope this will be a lesson to you."

"Oh, it will, Mommy, it will!" cried Basil. "I won't ever shoot my mouth off again."

"And don't go for walks," said his mother, "but keep close to the lake, where you'll be safe from the tyrannosaurus."

"In case he 'rex' you," said Herb, and plunged his head underwater again, while strings of bubbles rose as he laughed at his own joke.

"And if you want to grow up to be as big as your father," said Araminta, "there's one thing you must always remember to do."

"What's that, Mommy?" said Basil.

"Use your brains."

The Ugly Duckling

An ordinary farmyard duck once hatched a brood of ordinary ducklings. But when they were all free of their eggshells and scuttering about as newborn ducklings do, there was still one egg left in the nest.

It was a much bigger egg than the others had been, and the duck continued doggedly to sit upon it, hoping that it, too, would hatch—which, some days later, it did.

Soon the duck could see that this last child was unlike his brothers and sisters. He was larger, he was grayish where

they were yellow, and his legs and feet were bigger and his neck much longer than theirs.

The duck thought him quite beautiful and, proud mother that she was, she constantly told him so.

"You, my son," she said, day in, day out, "are beautiful. Your brothers and sisters are healthy, normal, ordinary ducklings, but you alone are beautiful," and she constantly showed him off to the other birds in the farmyard, the hens and the geese and the turkeys.

"Look at him," the old duck said to them, day in, day out. "Is he not the most beautiful duckling you ever set eyes on?"

Not surprisingly, after all this constant flattery, the beautiful duckling grew up to be extremely bigheaded.

He would stand by the duck pond and look at his reflection and say to himself, "Observe my noble body and my powerful wings and my great webbed feet and my long and elegant neck. What a truly beautiful duckling I am!"

And at last, to top it all off, his plumage, which had been gray, turned to a brilliant snowy whiteness.

One day the beautiful duckling left the duck pond and

made his way to a nearby lake. Here he stood by the water's edge and looked once more at his reflection.

"Without doubt," he said, "I must be the most beautiful duckling in the world. No other could compare with me."

Then he looked up and saw a whole flock of great white birds swimming on the surface of the lake—birds that looked just like him, birds that certainly could compare with him.

"Even so, they cannot be as beautiful as I," he said to himself, and he swam proudly out to meet them.

At the sight of this stranger approaching, the swans

banded together, arching their wings and hissing angrily.

"Who are you?" they cried, and the reply came, "Make way! I am the beautiful duckling."

"Duckling!" said one of the swans to the rest, and, "He's crazy!" said another. "And he's a bighead!" said a third, and then a host of voices said, "Let's duck the duckling!"

And with that all the swans set upon the newcomer.

They buffeted him with their wings, and pecked at him, and pulled out his tail feathers, and finally they ducked his head underwater.

Somehow he struggled back to the duck pond. He saw

the old duck who had hatched him so long ago, but now she did not recognize the battered, muddied bird, his neck limp, his wings trailing, his plumage all in dirty disarray.

"Who on earth are you?" she said.

"The beautiful duckling!" he gasped.

"A duckling you may be," said the old duck doubtfully, "but beautiful you are not. Sure as eggs is eggs, there's only one word to describe you: ugly!"

The Great Sloth Race

Dozy was a two-fingered tree sloth.

On his feet he had three toes, but on each hand only two fingers.

Snoozy was a three-fingered tree sloth. He also had three toes, but he had three fingers on each hand.

All tree sloths spend their lives upside down in the forests of South America. They are born upside down, they live upside down, and the only time they ever touch the ground is when they die (upside down) and fall off their perches.

Always they are facing the sky, so that they see only the

tops of the trees, and when it rains, only their tummies get wet.

Dozy and Snoozy were quite different, and not just because Snoozy had more fingers.

Dozy was grumpy. He had a bad-tempered expression. He would bite, and slash with his sharp claws.

Snoozy was gentle. On his face he wore what looked like a smile. He only waved his arms around and never bit anyone.

Dozy was brownish.

Snoozy was silvery.

Dozy was boastful.

Snoozy was modest.

Where they were alike was in the way they moved, and not just because it was upside down. It was also very, very slow.

All tree sloths are slow, but Dozy and Snoozy were among the slowest sloths in the whole of South America.

Snoozy didn't mind this.

"Nice and easy does it," he would say gently to himself as

very, very slowly he reached out with one three-fingered hand to pull himself forward.

Dozy did mind.

"Get a move on," he would say grumpily to himself as very, very slowly he reached out and pulled himself forward with one two-fingered hand.

The other creatures of the forest made fun of Dozy and Snoozy. The brightly colored macaws screeched with laughter at the tree sloths, and the monkeys hung by their tails right in front of the noses of Dozy and Snoozy and shouted, "Slowpoke!" at them. Dozy slashed at them angrily, but Snoozy only waved his arms around, while on his face he wore what looked like a smile.

One day, by chance, Dozy and Snoozy met.

Snoozy was hanging under a branch having a nap when Dozy came crawling along (upside down of course, and very, very slowly) underneath the same branch.

78

"Hey, you!" said Dozy loudly. "Get out of my way."

Snoozy woke up.

"Oh, sorry," he said softly, and he began to reverse. Now a sloth going backward moves very, very, very slowly indeed, and while Dozy was waiting, he noticed Snoozy's hands.

He's got three fingers on each, Dozy thought. Stuck-up creature. Snoozy noticed that Dozy had only two fingers on each hand. Poor guy, he thought.

"I suppose you think you're better than me?" said Dozy.

"Better?" said Snoozy. "What do you mean?"

"I suppose you think you're faster than me, because you've got extra fingers?"

"Oh, no," said Snoozy. "I wouldn't think so."

"We'll see," said Dozy. "I challenge you to a race."

By now Snoozy had reversed far enough to reach another nearby branch and thus get out of Dozy's way. He didn't want to race anyone, least of all this bad-tempered sloth.

But the monkeys had been listening, and they told the macaws, and the macaws flew all around the forest spreading the news.

"The Great Sloth Race!" they screeched. "Come on, come on, everybody, to see the Great Sloth Race!"

There was no way now, it seemed to Snoozy, that he could escape having to race Dozy.

It took a long time, of course, before all was ready, but at last Dozy and Snoozy were hanging upside down on two long branches that ran parallel to each other.

Then the judge, an old and wise toucan, opened his enormous beak and called, "Ready, set, go!"

Very, very slowly, one with a two-fingered hand, one with a three-fingered, Dozy and Snoozy reached out to pull themselves forward. After an hour they had traveled about halfway along their branches. Dozy was slightly ahead.

Many of the animals of the forest who were watching had become bored and had flown or run or crawled or hopped away. After two hours Dozy was well ahead and nearing the end of his branch.

By now everyone had become fed up with so slow a race, and all had gone away except the judge.

After three hours Dozy reached the end of his branch.

Opening his enormous beak, the toucan called, "Stop! The race is over."

Snoozy stopped.

"Told you so!" shouted Dozy. "I got to the end first. I was faster than him, even though I've only got two toes on each hand and he's got three. I've won the race!"

The old, wise toucan flew down and landed beside Snoozy.

"Oh dear," he said softly. "I should have explained the rules to Dozy. I'm afraid he went too fast. The object of a sloth race is to see who can go the slowest. Congratulations, Snoozy. You are the winner."

Upside down as always, Snoozy looked up at the toucan.

On his face he wore what looked like a smile.

Blessu

Blessu was a very small elephant when he sneezed for the first time.

The herd was moving slowly through the tall elephant grass, so tall that it hid the legs of his mother and his aunts, and reached halfway up the bodies of his bigger brothers and sisters.

But you couldn't see Blessu at all.

Down below, where he was walking, the air was thick with pollen from the flowering elephant grass, and suddenly Blessu felt a strange tickly feeling at the base of his very small trunk.

Shutting his eyes and closing his mouth, he stuck his very small trunk straight out before him and sneezed:

"Aaarchooo!"

It wasn't the biggest sneeze in the world, but it was very big for a very small elephant.

"Bless you!" cried his mother and his aunts and his bigger brothers and sisters.

For a moment Blessu looked rather cowed. He did not know what they meant, and he thought he might have done something naughty. He hung his head, and his ears drooped.

But the herd moved on through the tall elephant grass without taking any further notice of him, so he soon forgot to be unhappy.

Before long Blessu gave another sneeze, and another, and another, and each time he sneezed, his mother and his aunts and his bigger brothers and sisters cried:

"Bless you!"

They did not say this to any of the other elephants, Blessu noticed (because none of the other elephants sneezed), so he thought, That must be my name.

At last the herd came out of the tall elephant grass and went down to the river, to drink and to bathe, and Blessu stopped sneezing.

"Poor baby!" said his mother, touching the top of his hairy little head gently with the tip of her trunk. "You've got awful hay fever."

"And what a sneeze he's got!" said one of his aunts. "It's not the biggest sneeze in the world, but it's very big for a very small elephant."

The months passed, and Blessu grew, very slowly, as

elephants do. But so did his hay fever. Worse and worse it got, and more and more he sneezed as the herd moved through the tall elephant grass.

Every few minutes Blessu would shut his eyes and close his mouth and stick his very small trunk straight out before him and sneeze:

"Aaaarchoooo!"

And each time he sneezed, his mother and his aunts and his bigger brothers and sisters cried:

"Bless you!"

But though Blessu was not growing very fast, one bit of him was.

It was his trunk. All that sneezing was stretching it.

Soon he had to carry it tightly curled up, so that he would not trip on it.

"Poor baby!" said his mother. "At this rate your trunk will soon be as long as mine."

But Blessu only answered:

"Aaaarchoooo!"

"Don't worry, my dear," said one of his aunts. "The longer the better, I should think. He'll be able to reach higher up into the trees than any elephant ever has, and he'll be able to go deeper into the river, using his trunk as a snorkel."

"Ah, well," said Blessu's mother, "soon the elephant grass will finish flowering, and the poor little guy will stop sneezing."

And it did.

And he did.

The years passed, and each year brought the season of the flowering of the elephant grass that shed its pollen and made Blessu sneeze.

And each sneeze stretched that trunk of his just a little bit further.

By the time he was five years old, he could reach as high into the trees, and go as deep into the river (using his trunk as a snorkel), as his mother and his aunts.

By the time he was ten years old, he could reach higher and go deeper.

And by the time Blessu was twenty years old, and had grown a fine pair of tusks, he had, without doubt, the longest trunk of any elephant in the whole of Africa.

And now, in the season of the flowering of the elephant grass, what a sneeze he had!

Shutting his eyes and closing his mouth, he stuck his amazingly long trunk straight out before him and sneezed:

"Aaaaaarchooooooo!!!"

Woe betide anything that got in the way of that sneeze!

Young trees were uprooted, birds were blown whirling into the sky, small animals like antelope and gazelle were bowled over and over, larger creatures such as zebra and

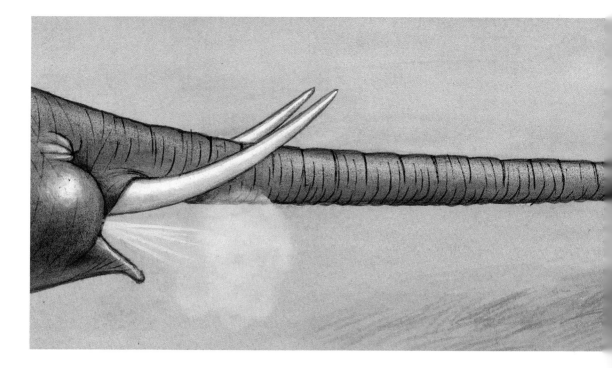

wildebeest stampeded in panic before that mighty blast, and even the king of beasts took care to be out of the line of fire of the biggest sneeze in the world.

So if ever you should be in Africa when the elephant grass is in flower, and should chance to see a great tusker with the longest trunk you could possibly imagine—keep well away, and watch, and listen.

You will see that great tusker shut his eyes and close his mouth and stick his fantastically, unbelievably, impossibly long trunk straight out before him. And you will hear:

"Aaaaaarchoooooo!!!"

And then you know what to say, don't you?

"Blessu!"

Hogsel and Gruntel

Once upon a time there were two little piglets, brother and sister, called Hogsel and Gruntel. They were very unhappy, for their mother had died and their stepsow was not kind to them, so they ran away, into the forest.

They walked and walked, side by side, until they were exhausted and it seemed that they must die from hunger.

But suddenly they came upon a little house all made of gingerbread, with windows of transparent sugar.

"Saved!" cried Hogsel, and he tore off a piece of the roof
and stuffed it into his mouth, while Gruntel helped herself
to a windowpane.

Just then an ancient crone appeared from inside the little
house.

"Come in, little pigs!" she cried. "You are hungry, I can
see, so I will heat up the oven." (And stick you both in it,
she thought—nothing nicer than roast pork!)

So Hogsel and Gruntel went inside, and the old crone heated up the oven.

"See if it's hot enough," she said. (And then I'll push you both in, she thought.)

"We're not tall enough to see into the oven," said Hogsel.

"You have a look," said Gruntel.

When the old crone did, they pushed her in and shut the oven door.

While she was cooking, Hogsel and Gruntel polished off all the rest of the little gingerbread house and its sugar windows too. All that was left standing was the oven, from which came a strong smell of cooking crone.

"I'm full," said Gruntel at last.

"Me too," said Hogsel.

"What about her?" said Gruntel.

"I couldn't eat another thing," said Hogsel.

So they left her to stew in her own juice.

The Septopus

From the moment he was born, Conrad believed himself to be an octopus. His mother was an octopus; his father was an octopus; all his many brothers and sisters were octopuses.

Conrad had no idea that he was different.

Until the day of the Graduation Parade.

Conrad's father was a rather strict octopus, and before his children left home to go and seek their fortunes in the great wide ocean, he always inspected them.

He lined them up: girls on the right, boys on the left.

"Present arms!" he shouted, and at this command they all held out their long, sucker-covered tentacles.

Then he swam slowly backward (as octopuses do) along the line, stopping before each child, his large unwinking eyes fixed upon its eight arms. Satisfied, to each in turn he gave the order "Dismiss!" and each jetted off (as octopuses do) into the wild blue yonder, waving good-bye with all its arms.

Last in line was Conrad.

"Present arms!" barked his father, and Conrad held them out. His father changed color (as octopuses do).

He turned a dark red.

"Come and look at this!" he called to his wife.

She came and looked.

She turned a bright blue.

"Oh, no!" she whispered. "He can't be!"

"Oh, yes!" growled her husband. "He is!" And then, instead of "Dismiss!" he shouted, "Disgrace!"

Conrad turned pale.

"Please, Father; please, Mother," he said. "What is the matter?"

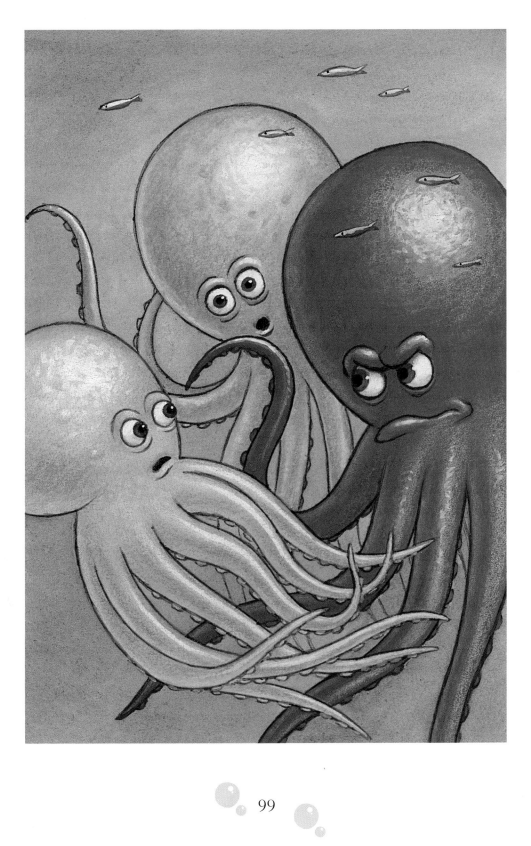

"Oh, Conrad," said his mother sadly, "you have only seven arms."

"You," said his father angrily, "are a septopus!" And then they each let out a cloud of black ink (as octopuses do) and jetted hastily away.

So ashamed was Conrad that for a long time he steered clear of all other octopuses. But he was a growing boy, and like most growing boys he was always hungry. Seven arms, he found, were still plenty for grabbing hold of

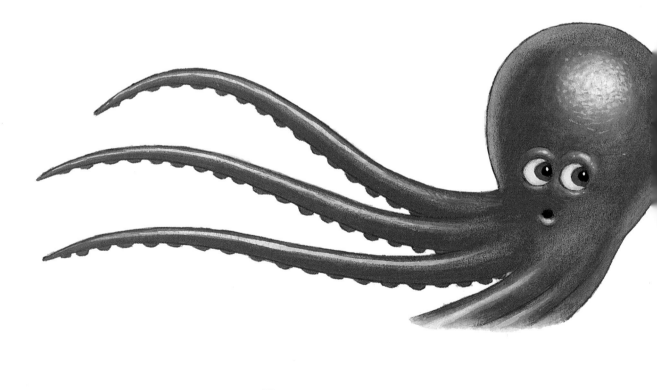

crabs and lobsters (as octopuses do) and stuffing them into his mouth, and he grew quickly.

But still, whenever he saw another octopus he jetted off backward as fast as he could. Till one day, because he wasn't looking where he was going, he bumped straight into something. Turning around, he saw that it was not only another octopus, but a female, and a pretty one at that.

Conrad blushed bright red.

"Sorry!" he gasped.

"Oh!" cried the female angrily. "Not another one!"

Another one? thought Conrad. Does she mean I'm not the only septopus? Are there other septopuses in the sea?

"Another what?" he asked.

"Another pushy boy," she said. "Barging into a girl like that. Next thing I know, you'll be putting an arm around me, and then the other seven."

"Oh, no," said Conrad. "I couldn't."

"You're all the same," the pretty female went on. "Always

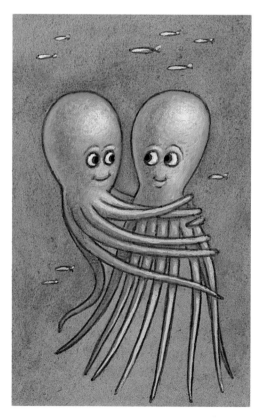

trying to cuddle a girl, can't keep your arms to yourselves. When I want a cuddle, I'll ask for it. And anyway, what d'you mean—you couldn't? Am I ugly or something?"

"Oh, no!" said Conrad. "You're beautiful."

At this the female octopus turned a delicate shade of pink.

"D'you think so?" she said.

"Yes, I do," said Conrad, "and I'd very much like to put eight arms around you, but I couldn't. You see, I'm sorry to say that I've only got seven. I'm not an octopus. I'm a septopus. I was born like that."

"Oh, you poor boy," said the female. "What's your name?"

"Conrad."

"I like that. And I like you, Conrad. You're not pushy like the rest. And you mustn't worry about having only seven arms. It makes you different from any boy I've ever met. By the way, I'm called Camilla. How d'you do?"

Camilla held out one arm, and Conrad grasped it with one of his, gently.

"I'm very well, thank you," he said. "In fact at this

moment I'm the happiest septopus in the sea."

"You're probably the only septopus in the sea," said Camilla, "and you're certainly the nicest. Give me a cuddle."

Carefully Conrad wrapped his seven arms around her.

"Oh, Camilla," he said. "Now that I've found you, I'll never let you go."

And then, arm in arm, they happily jetted away together.

Norty Boy

Hylda was an old-fashioned sort of animal. She did not hold with the free and easy ways of the modern hedgehog, and even preferred to call herself by the old name of *hedgepig*. She planned to bring up her seven hedgepiglets very strictly.

"Children should be seen and not heard" was one of her favorite sayings, and "Speak when you're spoken to" was another. She taught them to say please and thank you, to eat nicely, to sniff quietly if their noses were running, and never to scratch in public, no matter how many fleas they had.

Six of them—three boys and three girls—grew up to be well behaved, with beautiful manners, but the seventh was a great worry to Hylda and her husband, Herbert. This seventh hedgepiglet was indeed the despair of Hylda's life. He was not only seen but constantly heard, speaking whether he was spoken to or not, and he never said please or thank you. He gobbled his food in a revolting slobbery way, he sniffed very loudly indeed, and he was forever scratching.

His real name was Norton, but he was more often known as Norty.

Now, some mother animals can wallop their young ones if they do not do what they are told. A lioness can cuff her cub, a monkey can box her child on the ear, or an elephant can give her baby a whack with her trunk. But it's not so easy for hedgehogs.

"Sometimes," said Hylda to Herbert, "I wish that hedgepigs didn't have prickles."

"Why is that, my dear?" said Herbert.

"Because then I could give our Norty a good spanking. He deserves it."

"Why is that, my dear?" said Herbert.

"Not only is he disobedient, but he has taken to talking back to me. Why can't he be good like the others? Never have I known such a hedgepiglet. I shall be glad when November comes."

"Why is that, my dear?" said Herbert.

Hylda sighed. Conversation with my husband, she said to herself for the umpteenth time, can hardly be called interesting.

"Because then it's time to hibernate, of course, and we can all have a good sleep. For five blissful months I shall not have to listen to that impudent, squeaky little voice arguing, complaining, refusing to do what I say, and generally sassing me."

Hylda should have known it would not be that easy.

When November came, she said to her husband and the seven children, "Come along, all of you."

"Yes, Mommy," said the three good boys and the three

good girls, and, "Why is that, my dear?" said Herbert, but Norty only said, "Won't."

"Norty," said Hylda, "if you do not do what you are told, I shall get your father to give you a good hard smack."

Norty fluffed up his spines and snickered.

"You'll be sorry if you do, Dad," he said.

"Where are we going, Mommy?" asked one of the hedgepiglets.

"We are going to find a nice deep bed of dry leaves, where we can hibernate."

"What does *hibernate* mean, Mommy?" asked another.

"It means to go to sleep, all through the winter. When it's rainy and blowy and frosty and snowy outside, we shall all be fast asleep under the leaf pile, all cozy and warm. Won't that be lovely?"

"No," said Norty.

"Norton!" said his mother angrily. "Are you coming or not?"

"No," said Norty.

"Oh well, stay here then," snapped Hylda, "and freeze to death!" And she trotted off with the rest.

In a far corner of the garden they found a nice deep bed of dry leaves, and Hylda and Herbert and the six good hedgepiglets burrowed their way into it, and curled up tight, and shut their eyes, and went to sleep.

The following April they woke up, and opened their eyes, and uncurled, and burrowed out into the spring sunshine.

"Good-bye, Mommy. Good-bye, Daddy," chorused the six good hedgepiglets, and off they trotted to seek their fortunes.

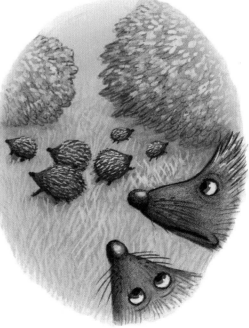

"Oh, Herbert," said Hylda. "I feel so sad."

"Why is that, my dear?" said Herbert.

"I should never have left our Norty out in the cold last November. He's probably frozen to death, poor little fellow. What does it matter that he was rude and disobedient and sassy? Oh, if only I could hear his squeaky voice again, I'd be the happiest hedgepig ever!"

At that moment there was a rustling from the other side of the pile of leaves, and out came Norty.

"Can't you keep your voices down?" he said, yawning. "A guy can't get a wink of sleep."

"Norty!" cried Hylda. "You did hibernate, after all!"

"Course I did," said Norty. "What did you expect me to do—freeze to death?"

"Oh, my Norty boy!" said Hylda. "Are you all right?"

"I was," said Norty, "till you woke me, nattering on as usual."

"Now, now," said Hylda, controlling herself with difficulty, "that's not the way to speak to your mother, is it? Come here and give me a kiss."

"Don't want to," said Norty.

"Anyone would think," said Hylda, "that you weren't pleased to see us."

"Anyone," said Norty, "would be right."

"Well, go away then!" shouted Hylda. "Your brothers and sisters have all gone, so get lost!"

"Won't," said Norty.

He yawned again, right in his mother's face.

"I'm going back to bed," he said. "So there."

At this Hylda completely lost her temper.

"I've had enough!" she screamed. "You're the rudest hedgepig in the world, and your father's the most boring, and I never want to see either of you again!" And she ran away as fast as she could go.

Herbert and Norty stared after her.

Norty scratched his fleas and sniffed very noisily.

"Looks like she's out of here, Dad," he said.

"Yes," said Herbert. "Why is that?"

"Can't think," said Norty. "But then, she always was prickly."

The Princess and the Pig

One day a beautiful princess was walking along a country road when she saw a large pig sitting on the grass.

Being of a kindly nature, she stopped to speak to it.

"Hello, piggy," she said with a smile.

"Hi," said the pig. "Though actually I'm a handsome young man. I upset the local witch, with the results you can see."

"What did you say to her?" asked the princess.

"I called her a dirty, smelly, ugly, evil old bag," said the

pig. "So she put a spell on me. 'Only a kiss from a beautiful princess can change things now,' she said, and off she went, cackling with laughter."

"Oh," said the princess.

She looked at the pig doubtfully.

But then, because she was of a kindly nature, she bent down and, shutting her eyes and screwing up her courage, planted a kiss on the end of the pig's rubbery snout.

Immediately the princess also turned into a pig.

Zap!

Of all the chameleons in Africa, Kenneth was the most unhappy. He couldn't change color.

Kenneth could do all the other clever things that chameleons do.

He could walk along a thin branch, holding it with two fingers of each hand.

He could roll his eyes in different directions at the same time.

He could shoot out his long, sticky tongue and, sometimes, zap a fly.

But his brothers and his sisters and his friends could do the cleverest thing of all.

They could change the color of their skins.

If they sat on a greenish leaf, they turned greenish.

If they sat on a reddish flower, they turned reddish.

If they sat on yellowish sand, they turned yellowish.

But Kenneth always stayed the same color—a sort of muddy brown.

However hard he tried, he didn't seem to be able to get the hang of changing. He was always muddy brown.

So he could only zap flies when he sat on brown mud.

So he didn't zap many flies.

He was the most unhappy chameleon in Africa.

One day Kenneth was sitting on a leaf, trying to zap flies. The leaf was silvery, so the flies could see him easily, and one after another they buzzed off, laughing.

"Oh, dear!" said Kenneth, rolling his tongue back up after the fifteenth miss.

"What's the trouble?" said a voice, and Kenneth looked around.

There on the next branch was a pretty young female chameleon, whose name was Kiki.

Kenneth sighed.

"I'm feeling blue," he said.

turned yellow; and to feel angry, and he turned purple; and to feel old and tired, and he turned gray.

"Now," said Kiki, "try feeling unhappy."

"No," said Kenneth, rolling his eyes. "Now that I've met you, blue's the one color I'm never going to be. Let's go fly zapping!"

And from then on the flies never had another chance to laugh at Kenneth the chameleon.

Zap! They never knew what hit them.

"You don't look it," said Kiki. "Why do you stay muddy brown on a silvery leaf?"

Kenneth was ashamed. He rolled his eyes in different directions.

"I can't change," he said. "All my brothers and sisters and friends can change color, but I can't get the hang of it. I wish I could. I'm green with envy."

"You don't look it," said Kiki again. "But," she said softly, "I'll tell you what you do look."

"What?"

"You look very handsome."

Kenneth felt terribly embarrassed.

"There!" she cried. "You can do it!"

Kenneth kept one eye on Kiki and rolled the other one backward to look at himself. He had turned bright red!

"You see," said Kiki, "you felt embarrassed, didn't you?"

"Yes," said Kenneth.

"Well, there you are. If you want to be green, for instance, try *feeling* envious."

So he tried and, sure enough, he turned green.

Then Kiki told him to pretend to feel frightened, and he